THE TRUCK ON THE TRACK

By Janet Burroway
Illustrated by John Vernon Lord

Copyright © 1970, 2011 by Janet Burroway and John Vernon Lord. 97082-BURR

ISBN: Softcover   978-1-4653-4034-4
       Hardcover   978-1-4653-4035-1

All rights reserved. No part of this book may be reproduced or transmitted in any form or by any means, electronic or mechanical, including photocopying, recording, or by any information storage and retrieval system, without permission in writing from the copyright owner.

This is a work of fiction. Names, characters, places and incidents either are the product of the author's imagination or are used fictitiously, and any resemblance to any actual persons, living or dead, events, or locales is entirely coincidental.

This book was printed in the United States of America.

To order additional copies of this book, contact:
Xlibris Corporation
1-888-795-4274
www.Xlibris.com
Orders@Xlibris.com

For

Jo, Timothy, Katie, Tobyn and Corin

The truck stuck on the track.

The Sheik got out and took a look.
The Sheik said, "Eek!
We're out of luck.
This truck is stuck.
This truck is broke.
We'll have to walk."

The Cook let out a shriek.
"Alack!
This is no joke.
We're on the track.
The train will smack our truck
And wreck it."

The Yak said, "Quick!
Don't stand and talk.
For all the time you're yakkity-yakking,
The train is coming clackity-clacking
Lickety-split along the track.
And that will be an awful whack!"

The Imp said, "Humph!
I'll scare the scamp.
I'll make him jump.
It's simple!"

The Imp jumped on a stump and stamped.

No luck.
The truck stuck.

The Cock said, "Awk!
This is a shock.
I'll try a trick.
Stand back!"

The Cock took up a stick and struck.
The Imp stamped.

No luck.
The truck stuck.

The Grump began to growl, "Grr-umph!
I'm in a temper!
I'll thump his bumper.
You mustn't pamper
The lazy lump."

The Grump raced up a ramp and thumped.
The Cock struck.
The Imp stamped.

No luck.
The truck stuck.

The Hawk began to shake and chuckle.
"He'll get to work or he'll get the sack.
You'd better duck
When I attack!"

The Hawk broke up a brick and chucked.
The Grump thumped.
The Cock struck.
The Imp stamped.

No luck.
The truck stuck.

The tramp began to slump
and whimper.
"I'm limp and damp.
My coat is rumpled.
My crumpet's crumpled.
This truck is cramped.
Let's camp."

The tramp jumped out
and set up camp.
The Hawk chucked.
The Grump thumped.
The Cock struck.
The Imp stamped.

No luck.
The truck *still* stuck.

The Doctor said, "I've got the ticket.
We mustn't treat the truck as wicked.
We mustn't mock and sock and kick.
He may be weak.
He may have an ache
Or a creak or a crack
Or a crick in his neck."

The Doctor picked up a book and looked.
The Tramp camped.
The Hawk chucked.
The Grump thumped.
The Cock struck.
The Imp stamped.

No luck.
The truck stuck still.

The Chimpanzee took up
his trumpet.
And said, "I'll make him skip
and romp,
'Cause I'm the Champ."
I know a tune called
'Tampa Trample,'
And when I pump it out
of my trumpet,
Just watch him scamper!"

The Chimp tripped up
and trumpeted.
The Doctor looked.
The Tramp camped.
The Hawk chucked.
The Grump thumped.
The Cock struck.
The Imp stamped.

No luck.
The truck stuck stock still.

The speckled Duck began to squawk.
The freckled Chick began to speak.
The Duck said, "Quack!"
The Chick said, "Duck,
That music makes my knuckles prickle.
It makes my knees begin to knock.
I makes my ankles start to tickle."

The Duck and the Chick did a bareback trick.
The Chimp pumped and the Doctor looked.
The Tramp camped and the Cock struck.
The Imp stamped and the Cook rocked.
The Yak gawked and the Sheik shook!

No luck.
The truck still stuck stock still.

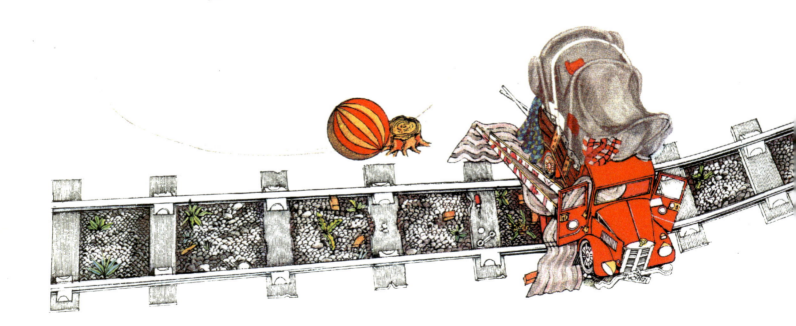

The train came.

Whack!

Tough luck.

Lightning Source UK Ltd.
Milton Keynes UK
UKRC01n0314200318
319719UK00003B/20